Philippe MATTER

MINI-LOUP
en classe de neige

HACHETTE
Jeunesse

Aller à l'école et en vacances en même temps, c'est possible !
Aujourd'hui, Mlle Biglu emmène tous ses élèves en classe
de neige.

Mini-Loup et Mini-Pic, très impatients à l'idée de partir
à la montagne, se retrouvent avec joie devant l'école
où le bus les attend. Ce n'est pas le cas de tout le monde !

« Comment peuvent-ils être contents de partir ! » s'étonne
Anicet, que l'idée de quitter son papa et sa maman rend
un peu triste.

Mais, vroum ! le bus démarre et, après quelques kilomètres
et plusieurs chansons, les chagrins sont oubliés.

« Youkaïdi ! Youkaïda ! » chantent en chœur tous les enfants.

Le voyage a été long mais, à l'arrivée, quelle récompense ! Le paysage est complètement blanc et la neige scintille sous le soleil ! La petite bande bondit hors du bus et commence une gigantesque bataille.

Vlan ! ping ! pang ! Les boules de neige volent de tous les côtés.

« Allons, allons, calmez-vous ! Je vous en prie… », ronchonne Mlle Biglu.

Dans « classe de neige », il y a le mot CLASSE ; ça veut donc dire qu'il faut aussi travailler un peu !

Mlle Biglu a le plus grand mal à faire la leçon, car Mini-Loup et ses amis n'ont qu'une seule ÉNORME envie : aller jouer dehors.

« Assis ! Silence ! Écoutez ! » bafouille-t-elle, désespérée,
tandis que Doudou perfectionne ses tirs d'avions.
« Youpi ! Réussi ! » s'écrie-t-il soudain, ravi.

Après le déjeuner, hop ! tout le monde se retrouve enfin sur les pistes, et ils n'ont pas l'air de rigoler autant que ce matin dans la classe !

« Pliez… plantez… tournez… pliez… plantez… tournez ! » répète inlassablement Mlle Biglu. Mais le ski, c'est drôlement plus difficile que la luge ! Si on ne glisse pas, on s'énerve, et lorsqu'on glisse, on hurle de peur !

« Au secours ! » crie Anicet en prenant de la vitesse.

Le brossage des dents terminé, les compagnons de la petite chambrée n'ont pas du tout sommeil ; c'est tellement rigolo d'être tous ensemble au moment de se coucher.

« Dépêchez-vous de dormir… Je veux entendre les mouches voler ! » avait prévenu Mlle Biglu en refermant la porte.

« Dormir ? Quel ennui ! » a murmuré Mini-Loup en jetant le premier polochon.

Plaf ! sploutch ! pif ! Le dortoir est transformé
en champ de bataille.

« Et que volent les oreillers ! » lance Eliot, le raton laveur
qui arbitre la partie.

Du haut de son lit, la chatte Muche compte les points
et semble captivée par le spectacle !

« Alerte ! V'là Biglu ! » s'égosille brusquement Doudou
qui faisait le guet près de la porte.

La porte s'ouvre d'un coup et Mlle Biglu apparaît,
une chandelle à la main. Elle a sa tête des très mauvais jours
et semble prête à crier, mais une drôle de surprise l'attend.
Tout le monde est sagement couché et dort... Enfin,
presque !

Du fond de son lit, Mini-Loup lance un clin d'œil complice
à son copain Mini-Pic.

Le lendemain, la leçon a lieu dehors. Mlle Biglu sort avec ses élèves pour observer les traces dans la neige.

« Là, ce sont les pas d'un merle, ici, ceux d'une belette…

— Et ça, c'est quoi ? demande Doudou en montrant de gros trous.

— Je ne sais pas du tout ! avoue Mlle Biglu.

— Moi, je sais ! s'exclame Mini-Pic. C'est Anicet qui a dégringolé ! »

Quelle rigolade !

Au bout de quelques jours, tout le monde sait à peu près skier.

« Aujourd'hui, nous allons faire une course de slalom, annonce Mlle Biglu. Suivez-moi, en avant ! »

Toute la petite bande s'élance à la poursuite de la maîtresse. Anicet prend rapidement la tête, mais Doudou a bien l'intention de le rattraper.

Seulement, au bas de la piste, Mlle Biglu a disparu.

« Ouh ouh ! Où êtes-vous ? demande prudemment Gus, le petit faon.

— Qu'est-ce qu'on va faire ? s'inquiète Anicet.

— On pourrait fabriquer un bonhomme de neige avec le gros tas qui est là-bas ! propose Anicet.

— Et pourquoi pas un Biglu de neige ? » suggère malicieusement Mini-Pic.

Mais à peine est-il terminé, que le Biglu de neige se met à trembler.

« A l'aide ! crie Maxou, le renard, en prenant ses pattes et ses skis à son cou.

— C'est peut-être un fantôme ? » bredouille le chien Wouf, figé sur place.

Sous la tête du Biglu de neige qui s'écroule apparaît alors celle de la vraie Mlle Biglu. Après une mauvaise chute, elle était tout bonnement ensevelie sous la neige.

Pour se remettre de toutes les émotions de la journée,
Mlle Biglu a préparé une énorme fondue au fromage.
La fondue, c'est amusant à manger parce qu'il y a toujours
des fils qui font des nœuds, et que, lorsqu'on perd
son morceau de pain, on a un gage.

« Ç'est drôlement bon ! salive le chat Baudouin.
— Deux à la fois, chè encore meilleur… », marmonne
Anicet, la bouche pleine.

La fin de la semaine est trop vite arrivée. Déjà, il faut retourner à la maison.

« Si l'école était comme ça toute l'année, je serais sûrement le premier de la classe ! dit Mini-Loup en entamant un concours de grimaces avec Anicet.

— Premier ex æquo ! » rectifie le cochon farceur.

Imprimé en France par I.M.E. - 25110 Baume-les-Dames
Relié par A.G.M. à Forges-les-Eaux
Dépot légal n° 8080 - Octobre 1999
22.71.3642.03/0
ISBN : 2.01.223642.1
Loi n° 49-956 du 16 juillet 1949
sur les publications destinées à la jeunesse.

ANIMALS Are NOT Like US

HORSES

For a free color catalog describing Gareth Stevens Publishing's list
of high-quality books and multimedia programs, call 1-800-542-2595
(USA) or 1-800-461-9120 (Canada). Gareth Stevens Publishing's Fax:
(414) 225-0377. See our catalog, too, on the World Wide Web: gsinc.com

Library of Congress Cataloging-in-Publication Data

Meadows, Graham.
    Horses / by Graham Meadows.
      p. cm. — (Animals are not like us)
    Includes bibliographical references and index.
    Summary: Describes the physical characteristics and behavior
of horses, pointing out ways in which they differ from people.
    ISBN 0-8368-2253-6 (lib. bdg.)
    1. Horses—Juvenile literature.   2. Horses—Physiology—Juvenile
literature. [1. Horses.]   I. Title.   II. Series: Meadows, Graham.
Animals are not like us.
SF302.M338   1998
636.1—dc21   98-18761

North American edition first published in 1998 by
Gareth Stevens Publishing
1555 North RiverCenter Drive, Suite 201
Milwaukee, WI 53212 USA

Original edition published in 1998 by Scholastic New Zealand Limited,
21, Lady Ruby Drive, East Tamaki, New Zealand. Original © 1998 by
Graham Meadows. End matter © 1998 by Gareth Stevens, Inc.

Printed in the United States of America

1 2 3 4 5 6 7 8 9 02 01 00 99 98

ANIMALS Are NOT Like US
HORSES

Graham Meadows

Gareth Stevens Publishing
MILWAUKEE

Horses are not like us.

They have four legs, not two.

Horses walk,   trot,

canter,   and gallop.

When they gallop,
they move very fast.

Horses are not like us.

Their feet are different from ours.

Horses have a special toenail, called a hoof, on each foot.

Some horses have metal plates, called horseshoes, on their feet.

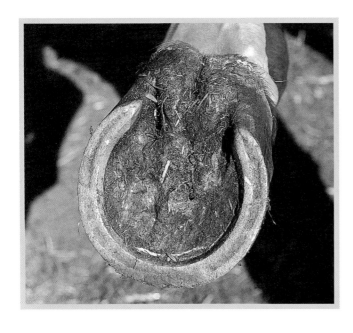

These protect the horse's hooves. Putting them on doesn't hurt the horse.

Horses are
not like us.

They don't
wear clothes
like we do.

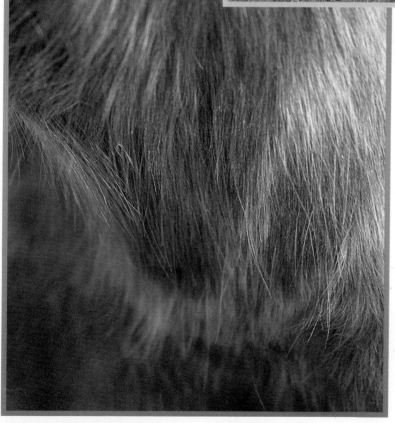

Horses' bodies
are covered
with a thick
coat of hair.

The long, coarse hair on a horse's neck is called a mane.

The long hair that falls over the forehead is called a forelock.

A horse also has a long, thick tail.

It uses the tail to swish away flies.

Horses are not like us.

They can see more than we can.

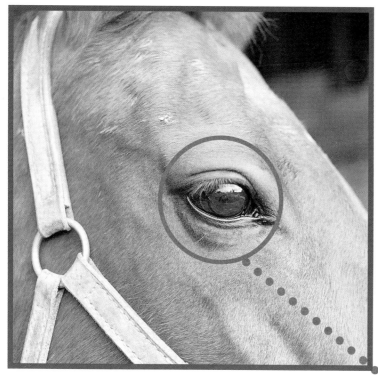

Their eyes
are on the
sides of
their heads.

They can
see what is
behind and
what is in
front of them.

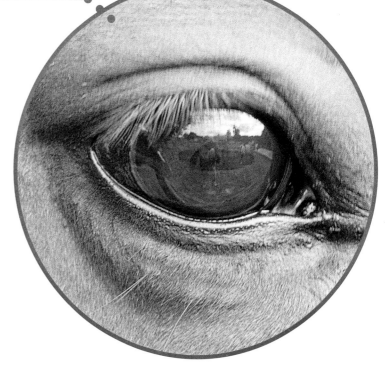

Horses are not like us.

They can move their ears
more than we can.

Horses can turn their ears to hear sounds coming from different directions.

Horses use their ears to show how they feel.

This horse is saying hello.

This horse is saying it's angry.

Horses are not like us.

They don't talk like we do.

Horses make a special noise that sounds like "neigh."

Horses are not like us.

They don't eat the same foods we eat.

Horses mainly
eat grass.

They use their
front teeth to bite
off the grass and
their back teeth
to chew it.

Some people
can tell how
old a horse is
by looking at
its teeth.

An old horse's
teeth are
worn down.

A small horse is called a pony.
Some children have their own ponies.

Ponies and horses are not like us.

Glossary

. . . .

angry — a condition of being upset with someone or something. *You can tell if a horse is **angry** by looking at its face and ears.*

canter — a slow and easy gallop. *Horses might **canter** around the ring at a horse show.*

coarse — rough in texture; not smooth and soft. *The hair of a horse's mane is very **coarse**.*

different — not the same. *There are many **different** kinds of horse breeds.*

direction — the line or course along which someone or something moves, lies, or points. *Horses turn their ears to hear sounds coming from different **directions** and places.*

forehead — the front part of the face above the eyes.

*The **forehead** of a horse slopes down.*

forelock — the long hair that falls over the forehead of a horse. *The color of a horse's **forelock** may be different from the rest of the horse's coat.*

gallop — a way that a horse runs when all four feet leave the ground. *When a horse **gallops**, it is running its fastest.*

hoof — a tough, protective covering of horn on the feet of some animals, such as horses, cows, and deer. *The foot of any of these animals is also called a **hoof**.*

horseshoes — the *U*-shaped metal plates that are fitted and nailed to the rims of a horse's hooves. *Some people believe that **horseshoes** bring good luck.*

mainly — for the most part. *Horses **mainly** eat grass, but they also eat oats.*

mane — the long, heavy hair growing from the neck and head of an animal, such as a horse or a male lion. *The **mane** of a horse is very coarse in texture.*

neigh — the long, high-pitched sound occasionally made by a horse. *A horse might **neigh** when it becomes excited over something.*

plates — pieces of strong metal, sometimes shaped in a special way. *Some horses have metal **plates**, called horseshoes, placed on their feet for the purpose of protecting their hooves. Putting the horseshoes on is the job of a person called a farrier.*

pony — a large, hoofed animal in the Equidae family that remains fairly small when fully grown. *A **pony** is under 14.2 hands high. A horse is over 14.2 hands high. One hand is equal to 4 inches (10.2 centimeters).*

protect — to keep safe from harm or injury. *Some horses wear metal horseshoes to **protect** their feet.*

swish — to move with a soft hissing or rustling sound. *Horses sometimes **swish** their tails back and forth to get rid of flies.*

trot — a four-footed animal's slow way of running in which the left front foot and the right hind foot move forward together; the right front foot and left hind foot also move forward together. *Horses sometimes **trot** at a horse show.*

worn — damaged or used up by long use, rubbing, or scraping. *The teeth of an old horse are often **worn** down from years of use.*

Activities

. . . .

Wild about Wild Horses
Find some books about wild horses and ponies at a library. Where do these horses or ponies come from? Where do they live? How do they find food and take care of themselves? What do they do when the weather is bad? Look at a map or globe to find the places where these wild horses and ponies live.

Baby Talk
You probably know that a baby horse is called a foal, but do you know what a baby pig is called? On a piece of paper, make a list of animals, such as horse, pig, lion, fox, and so on. Next to each adult animal's name, write the name, in parentheses, that its babies are called — for example, horse (foal), pig (piglet), lion (cub), fox (kit), and so on.

Show How You Feel
Some of the photographs in this book show ways that a horse indicates how it is feeling. Can you think of ways that other animals might show that they are afraid or angry, happy or sad? Draw pictures of the animals to illustrate the feelings. Like animals, people also have ways of showing their feelings. Act out a feeling to a friend and see if he or she can guess what feeling you are trying to show.

Helpers through History
Throughout history, horses have been doing valuable work for people almost everywhere in the world. Visit a local museum or historical society to learn about the ways horses have helped people, from long ago to today.

Books

The Complete Guides to Horses and Ponies (series). Jackie Budd (Gareth Stevens)

Great American Horses (series). Victor Gentle and Janet Perry (Gareth Stevens)

Horse Mania. Ed Radlauer (Childrens Press)

Horses. Jane Parker (Copper Beech Books)

Horses. Animal Families (series). H. D. Dossenbach (Gareth Stevens)

Magnificent Horses of the World (series). Hans-Jörg Schrenk (Gareth Stevens)

The Saddle Club (series). Bonnie Bryant (Gareth Stevens)

The Wonder of Wild Horses. Mark Henckel (Gareth Stevens)

Videos

Barnyard Babies. (Kimbo Educational)

Basic Horsemanship from the Ground Up. (Visual Education Productions)

Black Beauty. (Live Home Video)

Farm Animals and Their Mothers. (Phoenix/BFA Films & Video)

For the Love of Animals: Basic Horse Care and Ownership. (GCG Productions)

The Horse. (Barr Media)

Web Sites

homepages.ihug.co.nz/~
    meadows/animal.htm

www.bestfriends.org

Some web sites stay current longer than others. For further web sites, use your search engines to locate the following topics: *horse breeds, horse care,* and *humane society.*

Index

cantering 7
children 18

ears 14, 15
eyes 13

feet 8, 9
food 16, 17
forehead 11
forelock 11

galloping 7
grass 17

hair 10, 11
hearing 15
hooves 9
horseshoes 9

legs 6

manes 11

neigh 16

ponies 18

seeing 12, 13
sounds 15, 16

tails 11
teeth 17
toenails 9
trotting 7

walking 7

Former veterinarian Graham Meadows is the author and/or photographer of over seventy books for children about animals.

It was while working as a vet at the Aukland Zoo in New Zealand that Graham Meadows's interest in animal photography began. He finds the way animals look and behave endlessly fascinating. His desire to pass on this enthusiasm to a younger generation has led him to produce the *Animals are not like us* series for three- to seven-year-olds.